It was Grandma's birthday and for a special treat she had taken Katie to the art gallery. Katie loved the gallery because you never knew what you were going to see there.

"Look at the flowers in the paintings," said Grandma.

"I can only see blobs," said Katie.

"The pictures are made up of blobs," said Grandma.

"But when you stand back, the blobs make a picture."

Katie wandered off into the next room to try. There she
saw a painting called *The Luncheon* by Claude Monet.
When she stood back, Katie could see a garden.
'Grandma would love flowers like those for her
birthday,' she thought. She closed her eyes and
sniffed. She was sure she could smell the flowers.

And when Katie opened her eyes,
there she was, in the garden.
"May I pick some flowers?" she
asked a little boy.
He called to his mother, who came
and sat down to lunch with her maid.
"*Un bouquet*?" she said. "Why not.
Jean, you go and help her."
"Thanks," said Katie. "They're for
my Grandma."
"I sometimes pick flowers for my papa,"
said Jean. "He paints pictures of them.
Come and see . . ."

Katie AND THE
IMPRESSIONISTS

JAMES MAYHEW

ORCHARD

For my sister, the original 'Katie',
and a special thank you to Gabriel for helping
with the illustrations on page 32.

J.M.

ORCHARD BOOKS

First published in Great Britain in 1997 by Orchard Books

This edition published in 2014 by The Watts Publishing Group

7 9 10 8

Text and illustrations © James Mayhew, 1997/2014

The moral rights of the author and illustrator have been asserted.

A CIP catalogue record for this book is available from the British Library.

ISBN 978 1 40833 192 7

Printed and bound in China

Orchard Books

An imprint of

Hachette Children's Group

Part of The Watts Publishing Group Limited

Carmelite House, 50 Victoria Embankment London EC4Y 0DZ

An Hachette UK Company

www.hachette.co.uk

www.jamesmayhew.co.uk

Acknowledgements

The Luncheon: Monet's Garden at Argenteuil, c.1873 (oil on canvas), Monet, Claude (1840-1926) / Musee d'Orsay, Paris, France / Giraudon / The Bridgeman Art Library. *A Girl with a Watering Can*, 1876 (oil on canvas), Renoir, Pierre Auguste (1841-1919) / National Gallery of Art, Washington DC, USA / The Bridgeman Art Library. *Wild Poppies, near Argenteuil (Les Coquelicots: environs d'Argenteuil)*, 1873 (oil on canvas), Monet, Claude (1840-1926) / Musee d'Orsay, Paris, France / Giraudon / The Bridgeman Art Library. *At the Theatre (La Premiere Sortie)*, 1876-7 (oil on canvas), Renoir, Pierre Auguste (1841-1919) / National Gallery, London, UK / The Bridgeman Art Library. *Dancers in Blue, 1890 (oil on canvas)*, Degas, Edgar (1834-1917) / Musee d'Orsay, Paris, France / Giraudon / The Bridgeman Art Library.

Jean took Katie to a room full of pictures,
like a small gallery.
"This is Papa's studio," he said. "He's
a famous painter called Claude Monet."

"I'm good at painting," said Katie.
"Let's have a go."
They mixed the paint on palettes with
brushes and found canvases to paint on.
They painted portraits of each other
using blobs, just like real painters.

"Now I'd better get back to Grandma,"
said Katie.
"Will you come another day?" asked Jean.
"I'll try," said Katie. She picked up the bunch
of flowers and, waving goodbye, climbed
back through the frame into the gallery.

Katie saw that her flowers were beginning to wilt. "What I need is some water," she said, looking around the gallery.

She saw a painting called *A Girl With a Watering Can*, by Pierre-Auguste Renoir. Katie looked around her to make sure no one was watching, and climbed inside.

"May I have some water for my flowers?"
said Katie.
The little girl put the flowers into her
watering can.
"*Voila!*" she said. But the flowers still
drooped and flopped over.

"Come and pick some more!" said the girl.
So, Katie and the girl trampled through
the garden, picking flowers. Katie pretended
it was a jungle and that she was a panther
chasing the girl.

Suddenly, there was a terrible scream.
It was the girl's mother. "You have ruined
my garden!" she shouted.
"It wasn't me," said the girl, "it was her."
And she pointed at Katie.
"Come here, you naughty child," said the mother.
But Katie ran for the picture frame and leapt into
the gallery, leaving the flowers scattered behind her.

Katie sighed. She didn't dare go back to fetch the
flowers. She went to look at the other pictures.
There were a lot of pictures by Mr Monet.

Katie looked at one called *Wild Poppies*.
Wasn't that Jean, the painter's son, walking
through the field? Katie climbed in to see.

It was Jean! He was delighted to see her.
"We're going on a picnic!" he said, and
Jean's mother said that Katie could join them.
They walked together through the poppy field,
looking for somewhere to sit. Jean helped Katie
gather armfuls of poppies for Grandma.

Then, they sat in the shade of a tree – the perfect
place for a picnic. Mrs Monet opened
a bag. She had bread and cheese and strawberries.
But Jean heard a buzzing noise and looked up.
A black cloud of bees was flying towards them.

"They're after my poppies!" shouted Katie.
Jean and his mother ran into the poppy field.
But Katie ran to the picture frame and dived into
the gallery.

The bees followed Katie, who ran on and on until
she reached a window. She flung it open and
threw the poppies out. The bees flew after them.
Katie still didn't have any flowers for Grandma!

She saw another picture by Pierre-Auguste Renoir
called *At the Theatre*. It showed a girl holding
a posy of flowers.
"Grandma would love a posy like that," said
Katie, jumping into the picture.

"May I have your flowers?" asked Katie. "I'll swap my hair ribbon."

"Hush," said the girl. "The ballet is about to begin!"

Katie looked for a seat, but they were all full. The theatre manager appeared.

"*Mademoiselle*, may I see your ticket?" he said.

Katie didn't have one, so
she ran off down some steps.
She could hear the manager
coming after her and Katie ran
into a room to hide. It was full of
people in colourful costumes who
shouted at Katie, so she ran away
from them, towards some bright
lights and the sound of music.

Katie pushed past heavy velvet curtains and found
herself on stage. The dancers held their breath.
So did the musicians in the orchestra. So did
the audience. What was Katie going to do?

Katie danced! The music started up again and Katie
pranced all around the stage.
How the audience loved her! They had never seen anyone dance
so strangely before. They cheered and clapped and threw flowers.
Hundreds of flowers fell upon Katie as she twirled around.

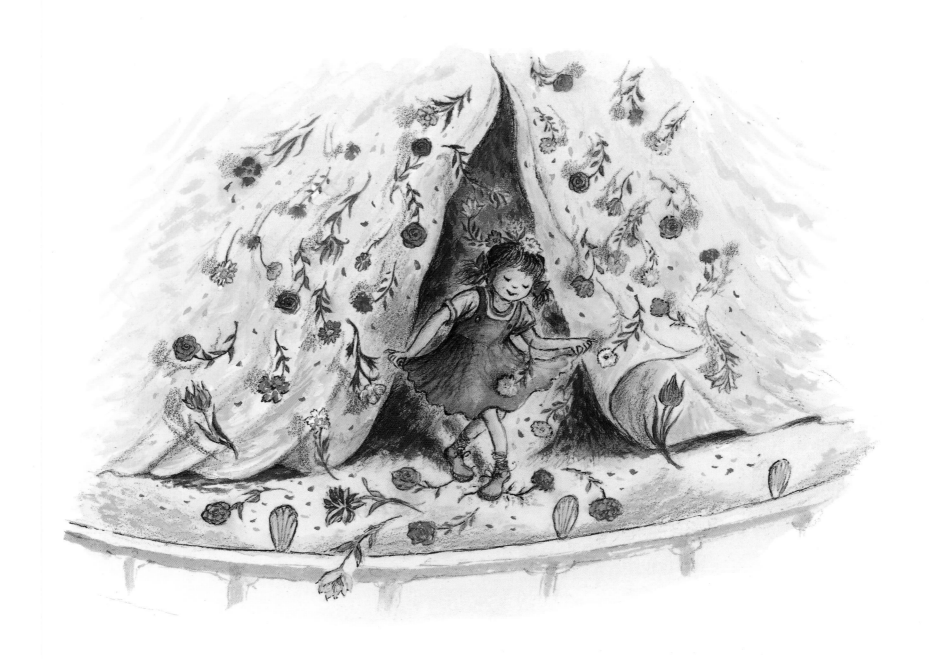

"Well done!" the audience shouted. "*Bravo!*"
When the music stopped, Katie curtsied
and gathered up her flowers.

The manager rushed over to her. "My dear, you
have such talent!"
Katie blushed. "I just jumped around a bit really," she said.
"You must dance every night; you will be famous!"
said the manager.
"Thanks, but it's Grandma's birthday," said Katie.
"I must get back."

Backstage, Katie saw a frame leading to the gallery.
"That's not the frame I came through," she said.
"These dancers must be in a different picture by another artist. I wonder which one?"
She gathered up her bouquet and climbed through the frame into the gallery.

Katie looked back at the picture. *Dancers in Blue* by
Edgar Degas, she read. "I wonder if I would have been
painted if I had stayed still long enough!" she said.
Then Katie ran over to her grandma and gave her
the flowers. "Happy birthday, Grandma!"

"Oh, I say!" said Grandma. "Wherever did you get these lovely flowers?"

Katie laughed. But what was that in her pocket? It was a paintbrush! 'Mr Monet will need that,' she thought. She ran back to the first picture, left the brush on the frame, and then ran to catch up with her grandma.

Get creative with Katie!

I've had a go at painting my own Impressionist pictures
– I hope you like them!

Impressionist artists painted really fast, and their pictures
look as though they are almost alive! So I tried painting
fast too, with blobs of colour. Sometimes the Impressionists
painted pictures outside. These are called 'landscapes'.
But you can paint almost anything you want!

Fill your paper with colour. Think big and remember
to stand back to admire your picture when it
is finished. I bet it will look amazing.
Have fun!

Love Katie x